JUNGLE SCOUT
A VIETNAM WAR STORY

by Tim Hoppey

illustrated by
Ramon Espinoza

Librarian Reviewer
Laurie K. Holland
Media Specialist (National Board Certified), Edina, MN
MA in Elementary Education, Minnesota State University, Mankato

Reading Consultant
Elizabeth Stedem
Educator/Consultant, Colorado Springs, CO
MA in Elementary Education, University of Denver, CO

STONE ARCH BOOKS
www.stonearchbooks.com

Graphic Flash is published by Stone Arch Books,
A Capstone Imprint
1710 Roe Crest Drive
North Mankato, Minnesota 56003
www.capstonepub.com

Library of Congress Cataloging-in-Publication Data
Hoppey, Tim.
Jungle Scout: A Vietnam War Story / by Tim Hoppey; illustrated by Ramon Espinoza.
p. cm. — (Graphic Flash)
ISBN 978-1-4342-0747-0 (library binding : alk. paper)
ISBN 978-1-4342-0846-0 (pbk. : alk. paper)
1. Vietnam War,1961–1975—Juvenile fiction. [1. Vietnam War,1961–1975—Fiction. 2. Vietnam—History—1945–1975—Fiction. 3. War—Fiction. 4. Jungles—Fiction. 5. Friendship—Fiction.] I. Espinoza, Ramon, ill. II. Title.
PZ7.H7794Ju 2009
[Fic]—dc22 2008006668

Summary: Sixteen-year-old Lam Hung was once a member of the Viet Cong. Now he's a Kit Carson Scout for the U.S. Marines, ordered to steer the troops safely around explosive land mines and deadly booby traps. One mistake could mean their lives. Lam's most difficult task could be getting the platoon to trust him, a former enemy.

Art Director: Heather Kindseth
Graphic Designer: Brann Garvey

Printed in the United States 5139

TABLE OF CONTENTS

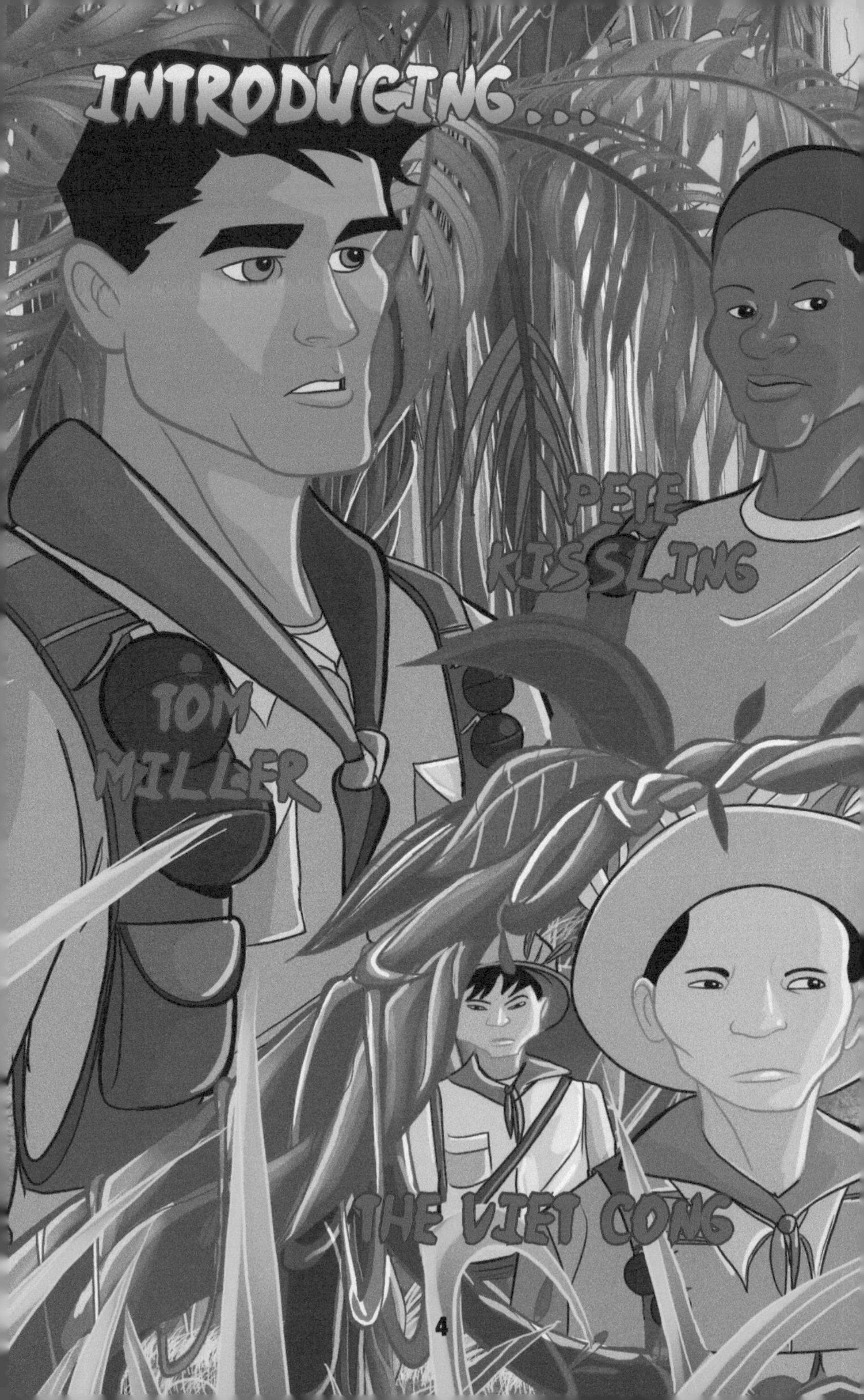
INTRODUCING...
PETE KISSLING
TOM MILLER
THE VIET CONG

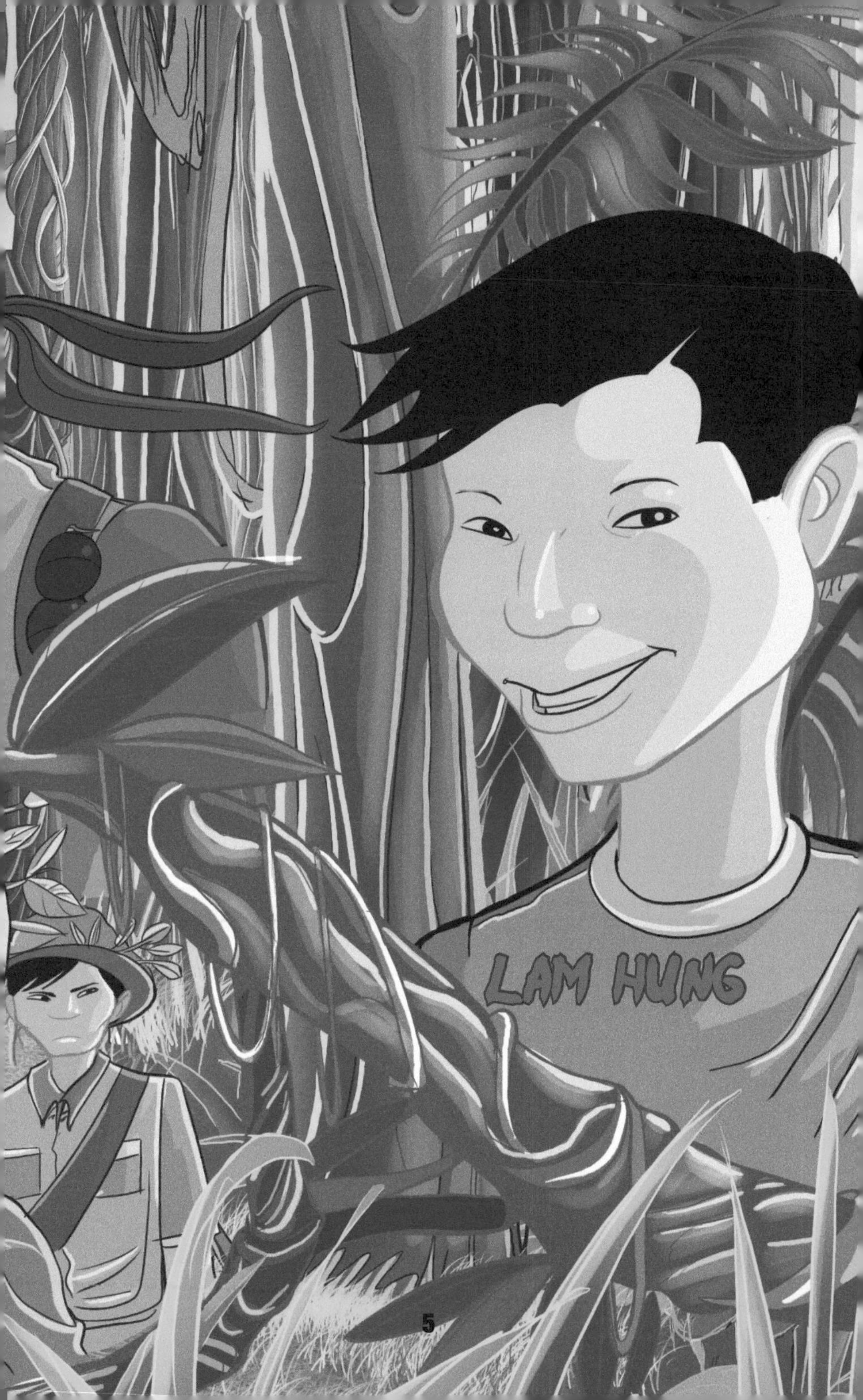
LAM HUNG

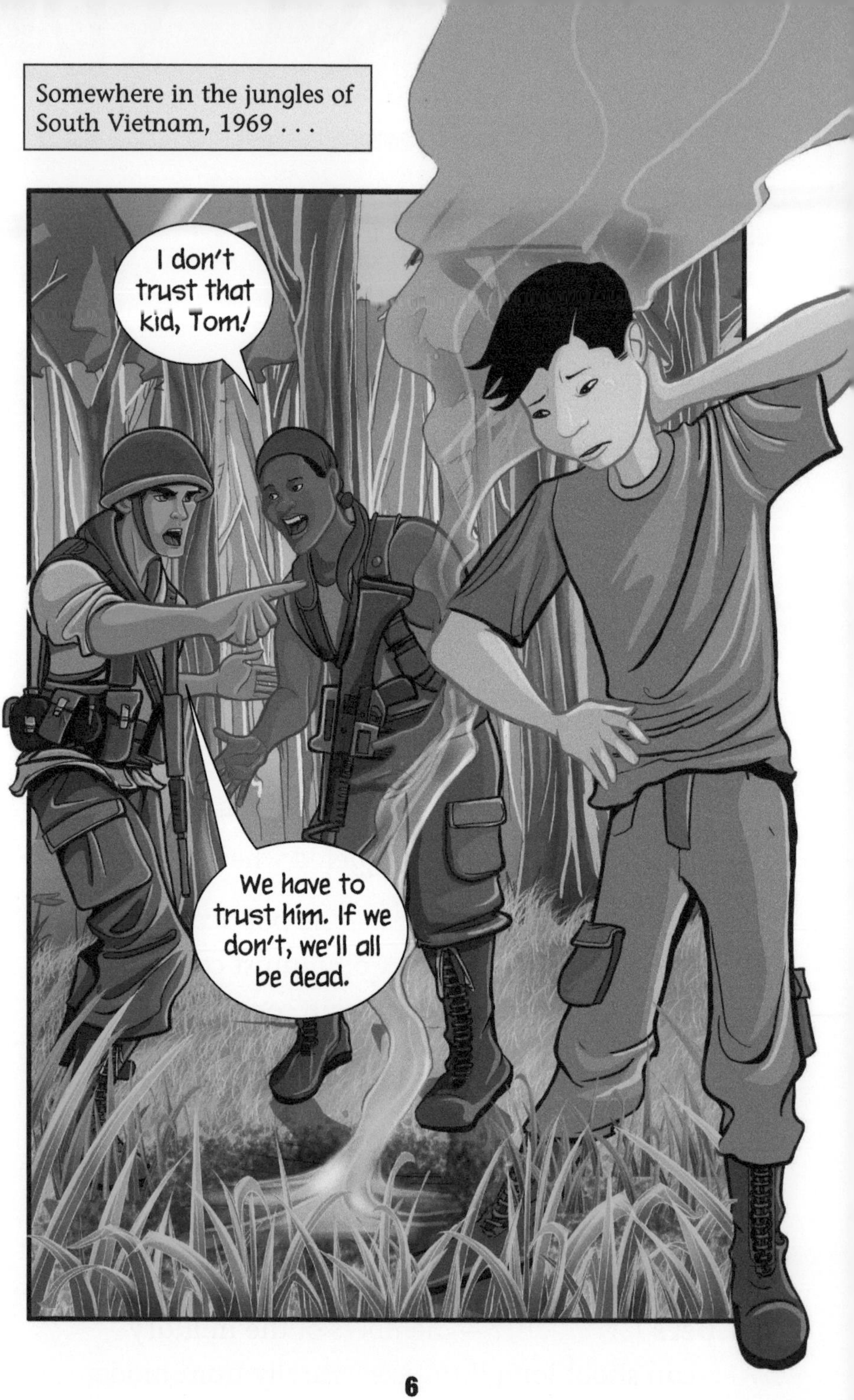
Somewhere in the jungles of South Vietnam, 1969 . . .
I don't trust that kid, Tom!
We have to trust him. If we don't, we'll all be dead.

Chapter 1

BAD LUCK

One member of the platoon had already died. He had stepped on a land mine. The soldiers were lucky that others weren't hurt in the explosion.

Sixteen-year-old Lam Hung was mad at himself. It was his job to spot danger. He was mad that he hadn't seen the land mine hidden in the dirt. Lam Hung hoped the American soldiers knew that they could trust him. He wouldn't let the same mistake happen again.

"Next time, it could be any one of us!" Pete warned the platoon. He knew Lam Hung spoke a few words of English, but he didn't care if the kid understood. Pete did not like the Vietnamese boy.

"I'll take that chance," Tom spoke up.

Lam Hung had been in the jungle for months with the American platoon. He was a Kit Carson Scout for the U.S. Marines and leading them toward the enemy, the Viet Cong. Lam Hung had once been a member of the Viet Cong forces. He had fought to make North and South Vietnam one Communist country. Now as a member of the U.S. military, he was trying to stop that from happening.

The platoon picked up their gear, and Lam Hung led them deeper into the jungle. Pete, Tom, and the rest of the soldiers spread out in case one of them stepped on a mine.

Suddenly, Lam Hung heard noises in the trees ahead. He held up his hand. The entire platoon froze in their tracks.

"What is it, kid?" Pete whispered. The soldiers never called Lam Hung by his name. They always called him kid or boy.

His name was odd to the Americans. But in Vietnam, every name had meaning. Lam meant forest, and Hung meant hero. Lam Hung thought it was a good name, although he didn't feel much like a hero at the moment.

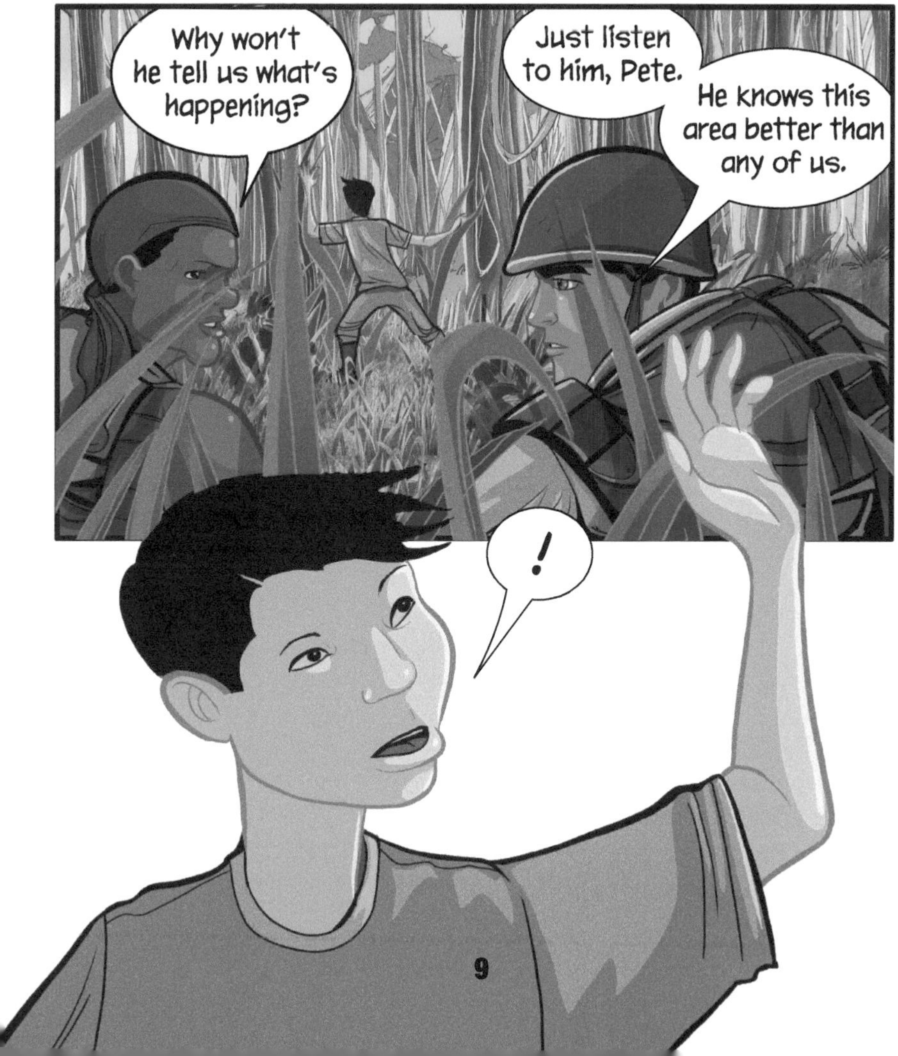
Why won't he tell us what's happening?
Just listen to him, Pete.
He knows this area better than any of us.
!

Lam Hung kept his hand up to halt the Americans. He closed his eyes and listened. Hung was born in this jungle, and he knew its every breath. He knew the sounds of its animals. He also knew the sounds of the enemy.

After a moment, the noises stopped. Lam Hung crouched down and slowly moved ahead through the jungle grass. He waved for the other platoon members to follow.

"Once Viet Cong, always Viet Cong," Pete said. "These Kit Carson Scouts can't be trusted."

"He's saved us a few times already," Tom replied. "He's steered us around dozens of mines."

"How does he know where the mines are?" Pete asked. "He's Viet Cong, that's how."

Pete knew he didn't have a choice. He picked up his rifle and followed Lam Hung. Then suddenly, noises returned from the trees.

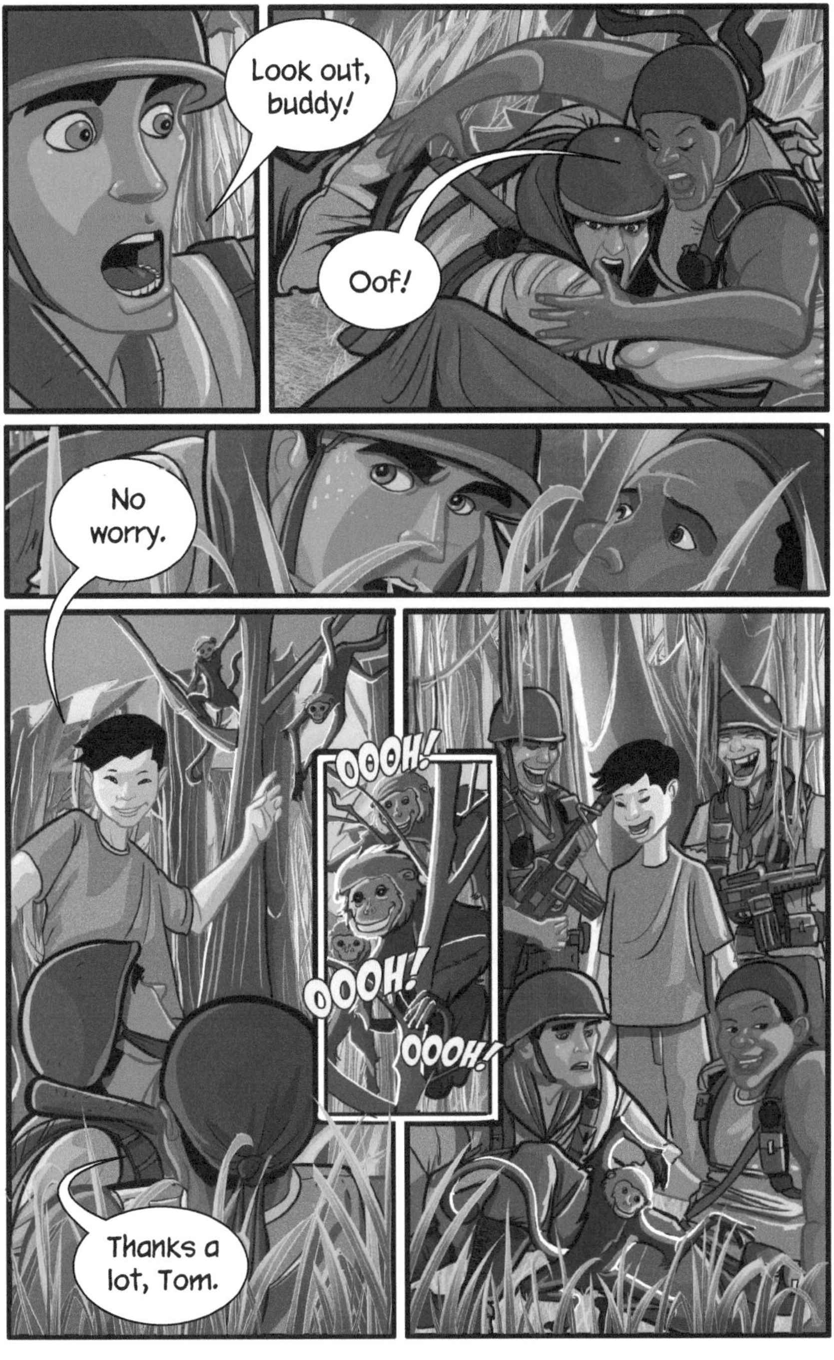
Look out, buddy!
Oof!
No worry.
OOOH!
OOOH!
OOOH!
Thanks a lot, Tom.

Chapter 2

TROUBLE AHEAD

Laughter in the jungle lasted only a moment. Lam Hung had a job to do. He would not make another mistake. Bent low to the ground, he continued walking. He heard the Americans follow behind him. They moved through the jungle like a herd of wounded elephants.

Lam Hung turned around, hoping to quiet down the troops. Just then, he saw an empty soda can on the trail. One of the platoon members was going to kick it.

"Number ten!" Hung shouted.

Pete watched Lam Hung rush toward the soldier. He knew "number ten" meant danger and "number one" meant complete safety.

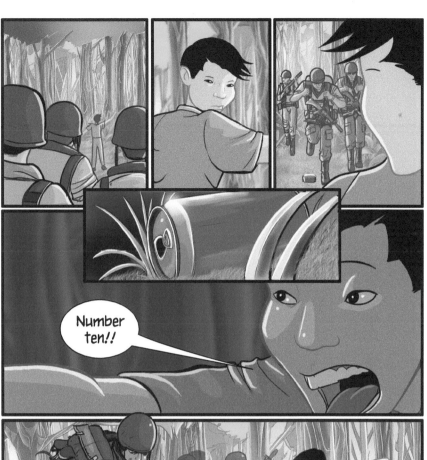

Number ten!!

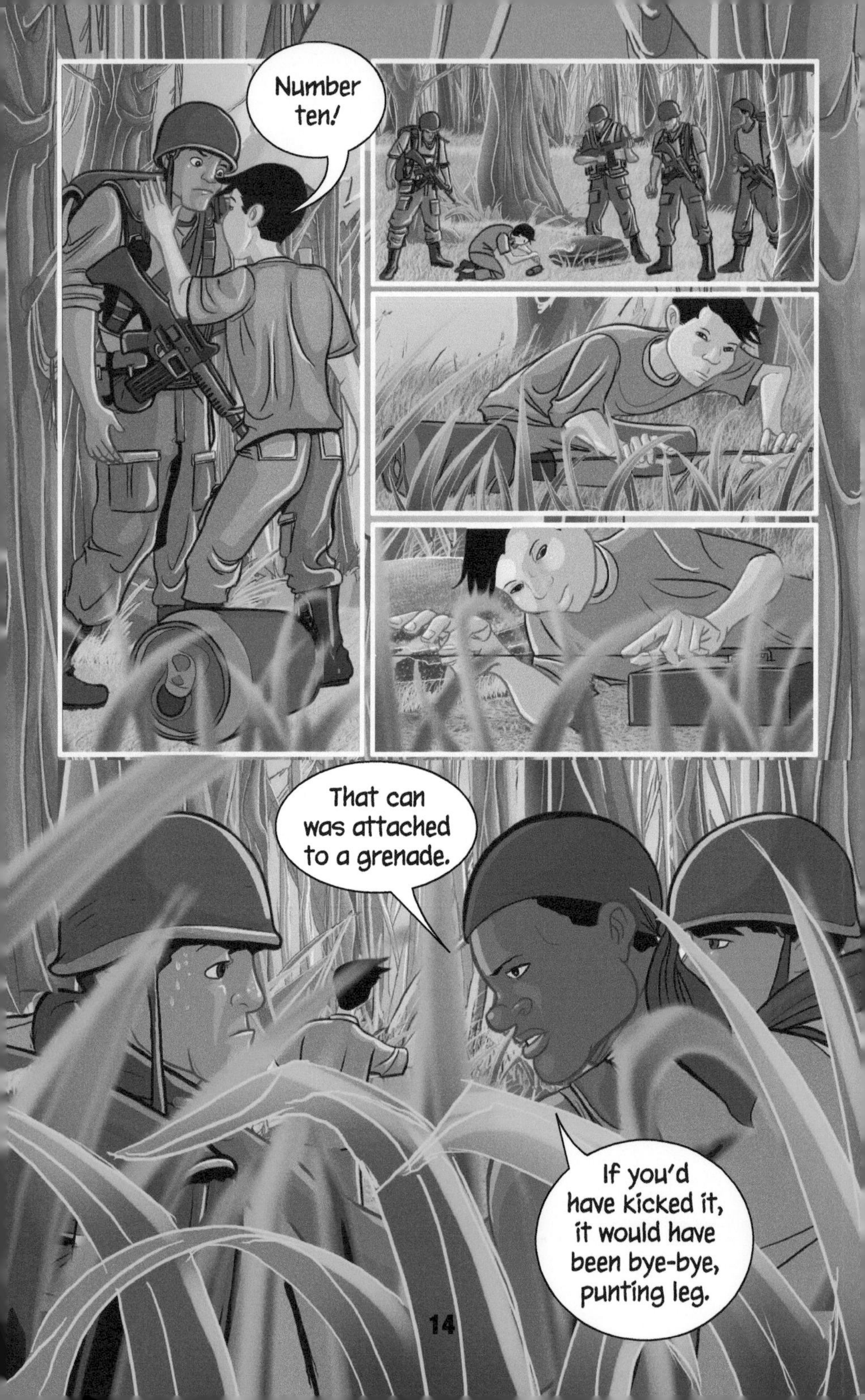
Number ten!
That can was attached to a grenade.
If you'd have kicked it, it would have been bye-bye, punting leg.

The soldiers watched the kid carefully take the trap apart. Then he waved them on and started forward again.

"How did he know there was a grenade in that can?" Pete grumbled.

"He's smart," Tom said. "He knows this jungle, and he knows the Viet Cong."

"Do you even know where we are?" Pete asked as they walked on. The jungle was getting thicker, and the air stickier.

"No idea," Tom replied. "Jack had the map."

"Right," Pete said. He thought briefly about their friend Jack, the soldier they lost when the kid missed that mine. Pete couldn't let himself think about Jack for long. In war, a soldier can't take time to think about lost friends.

"I'm starved," Pete said. "Hey, kid! We're going to eat now, okay?"

Hung turned around. The Americans were yelling at him again, making more noise. *The Viet Cong would hear them,* he thought. Pete was waving a can of beans and ham. Time to stop for lunch again.

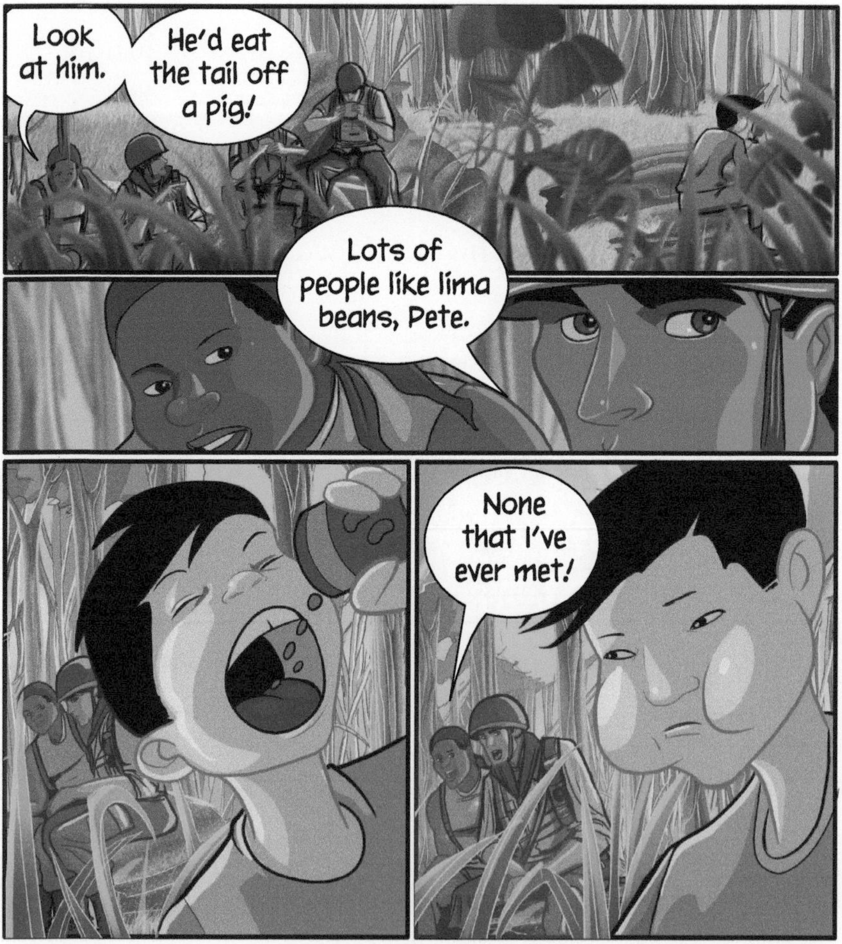
Look at him.
He'd eat the tail off a pig!
Lots of people like lima beans, Pete.
None that I've ever met!

Hung scooped the beans into his mouth. He was hungry after the morning's march. The last time they'd stopped for lunch, he hadn't gotten any rations.

Besides, it was nice to eat something other than plain rice. Lately, with the war on, it was hard even to get rice anymore.

When Hung finished his lunch, he dug a small hole and dropped the empty can inside. Then he gathered the other soldiers' trash and buried that, as well.

The American soldiers didn't know the Viet Cong like Hung did. They didn't know that the VC would find this trash. They would make mines from the empty cans. They would use the soldiers' trash to fight against them.

Lam Hung knew about mines, and he knew the jungle. But the VC knew even better.

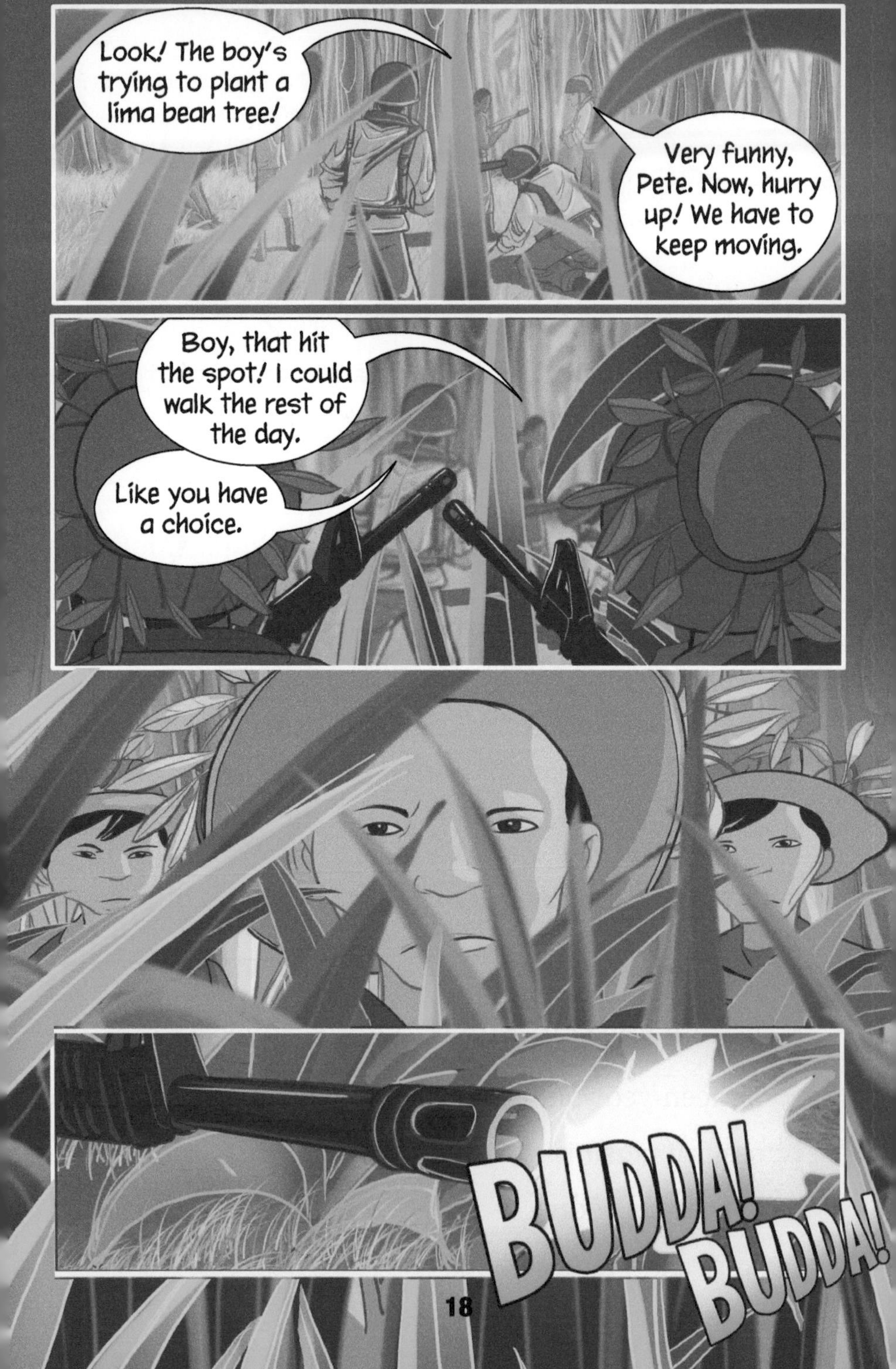
Look! The boy's trying to plant a lima bean tree!
Very funny, Pete. Now, hurry up! We have to keep moving.
Boy, that hit the spot! I could walk the rest of the day.
Like you have a choice.
BUDDA! BUDDA!

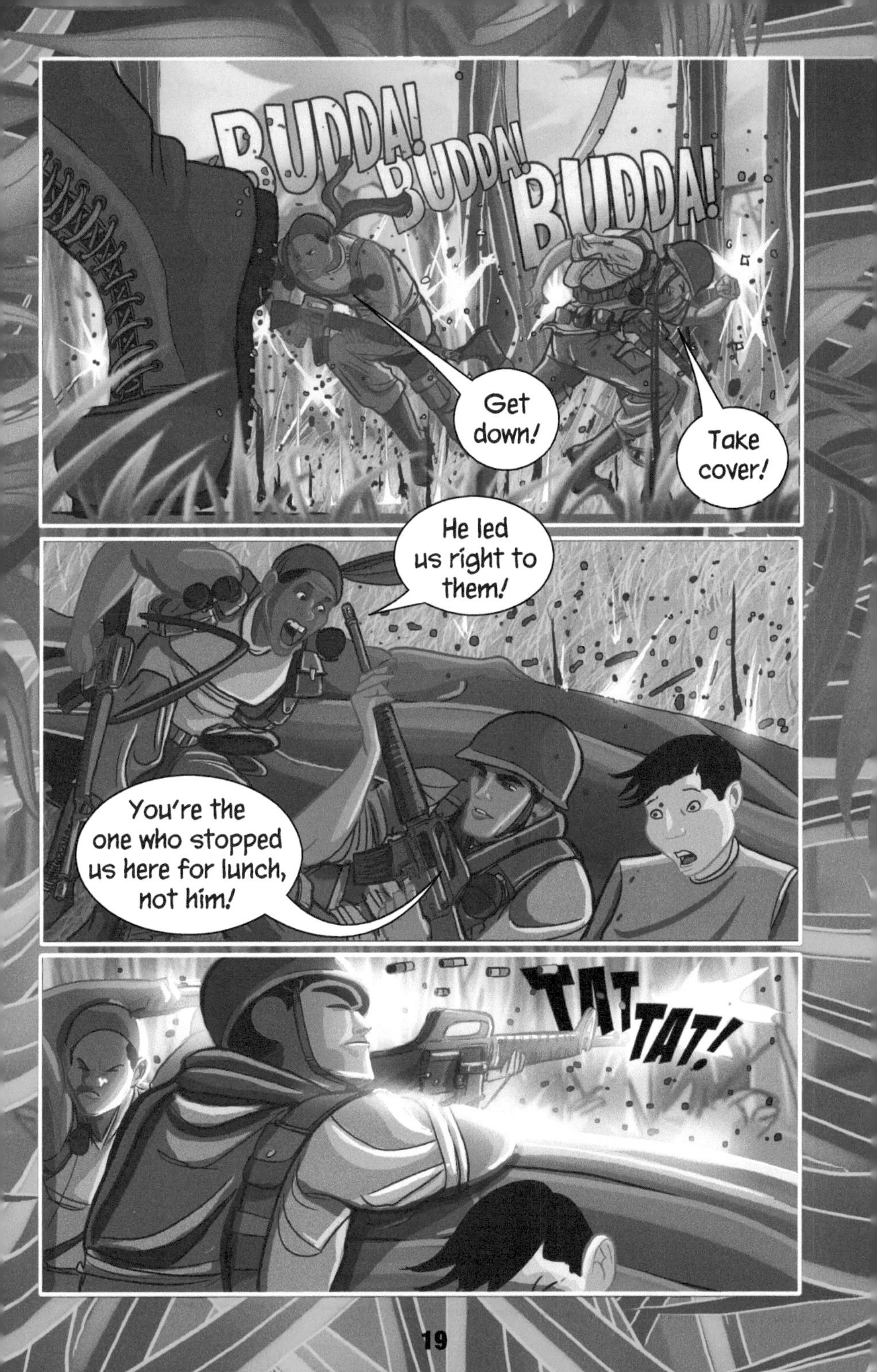
BUDDA! BUDDA! BUDDA!
Get down!
Take cover!
He led us right to them!
You're the one who stopped us here for lunch, not him!
TAT TAT!

Soon the gunfire stopped. When the kid got up on his knees, the soldiers did too.

"Where did the shots come from? Did you see which way?" Tom asked.

"I never do," Pete replied, standing up. The kid was crouched nearby, motioning for the soldiers to follow.

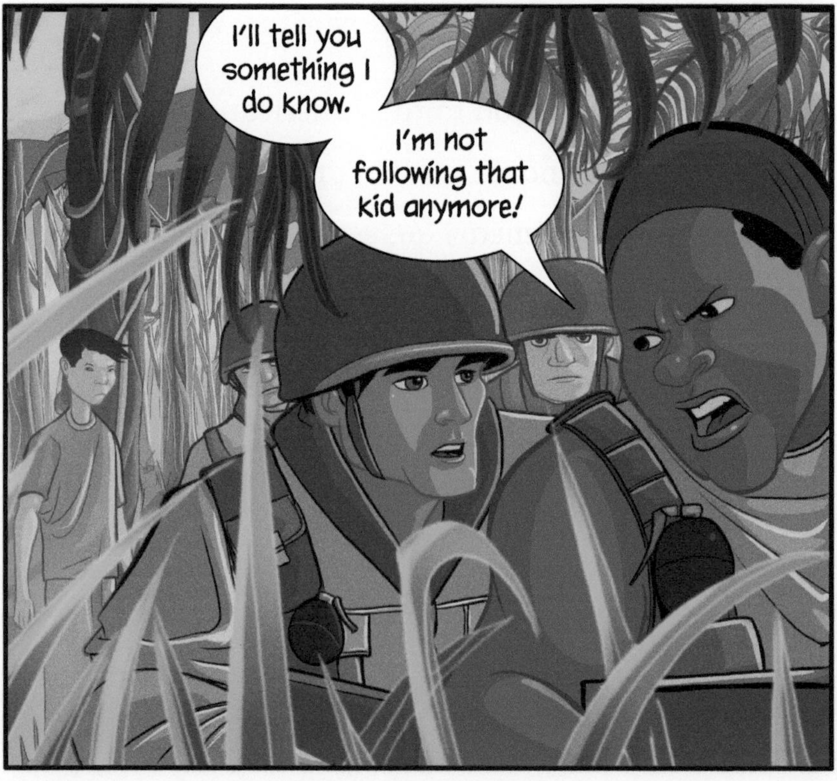
I'll tell you something I do know.
I'm not following that kid anymore!

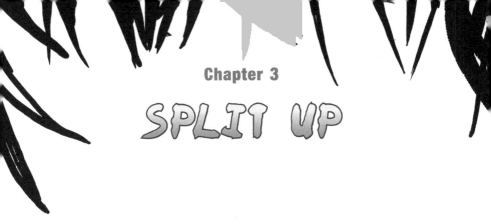

Chapter 3

SPLIT UP

Lam Hung waved at the soldiers. If they didn't move soon, the Viet Cong would surround them and the mission would be over.

The Americans didn't follow. They were yelling at each other. Pete was mad, and he was glaring at Hung.

Hung kept signaling to move forward. After a moment, Pete got on his belly and crawled off in the other direction.

"Come on, Tom," Pete shouted as he moved through the brush. "Let's go!"

Tom glanced at the kid. He was still waving them on. "The kid says we should go that way," he said.

"Forget the kid," Pete said. "He's Viet Cong, and there's nothing that way but more traps, more snipers, and more VC."

Pete crawled on. Tom couldn't let his partner go off into the jungle alone. They had to stick together. He took one more glance at the kid, then scurried off behind Pete.

Hung watched the soldiers as they crawled off in the other direction. *Were they crazy?* he wondered. The Viet Cong were gathering over there, preparing to circle around the platoon.

Hung couldn't let them go that way. He couldn't let these Americans die.

After Pete had crawled a few yards into the thick growth, he still hadn't heard any more shots. He got to his feet.

"Let's move," he called to his partner. Tom got up too, and they began to run.

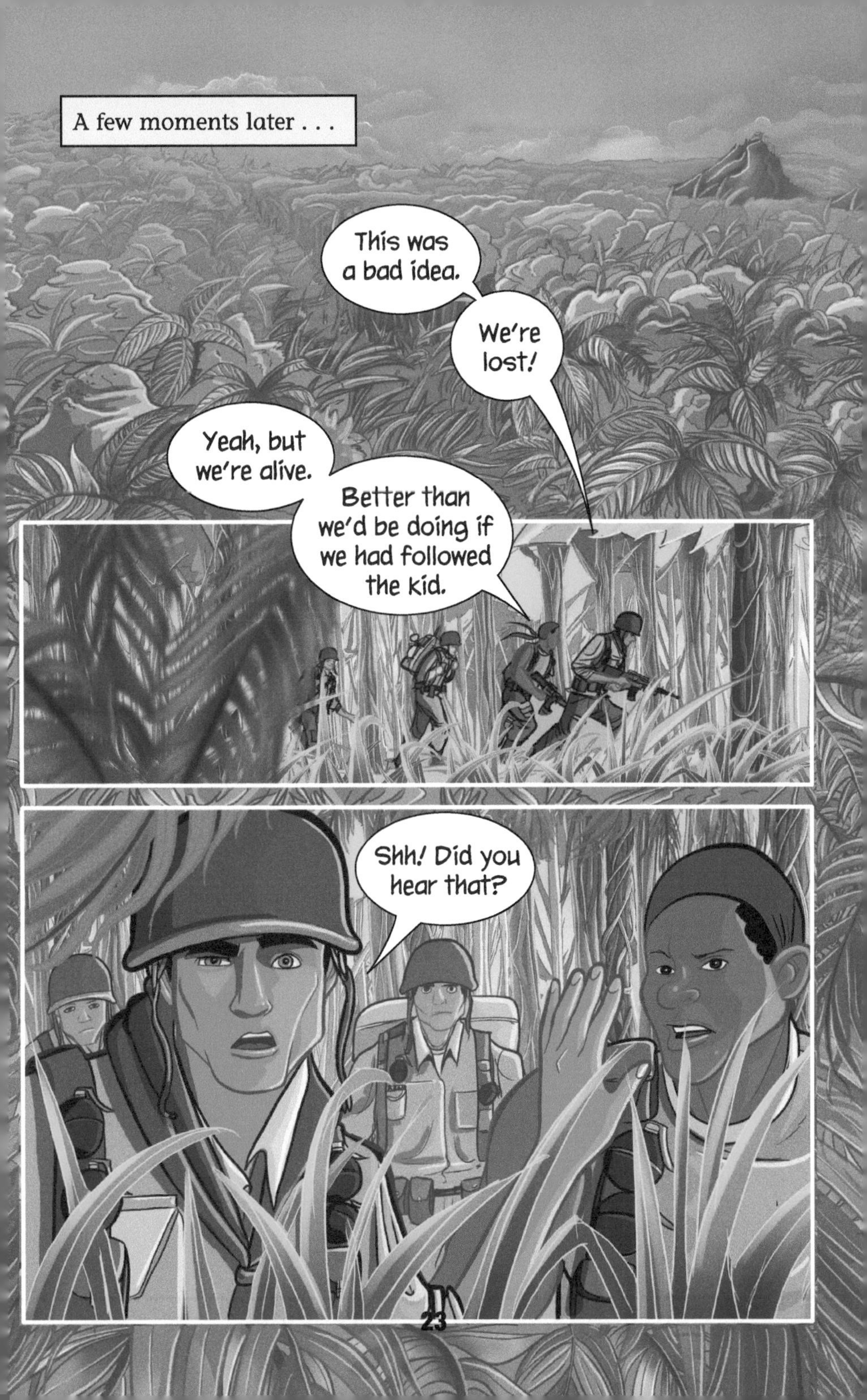
A few moments later . . .
This was a bad idea.
We're lost!
Yeah, but we're alive.
Better than we'd be doing if we had followed the kid.
Shh! Did you hear that?

Suddenly, Tom dropped to the ground, and then pulled Pete down by the wrist. "That tree moved," Tom said, as quietly as he could.

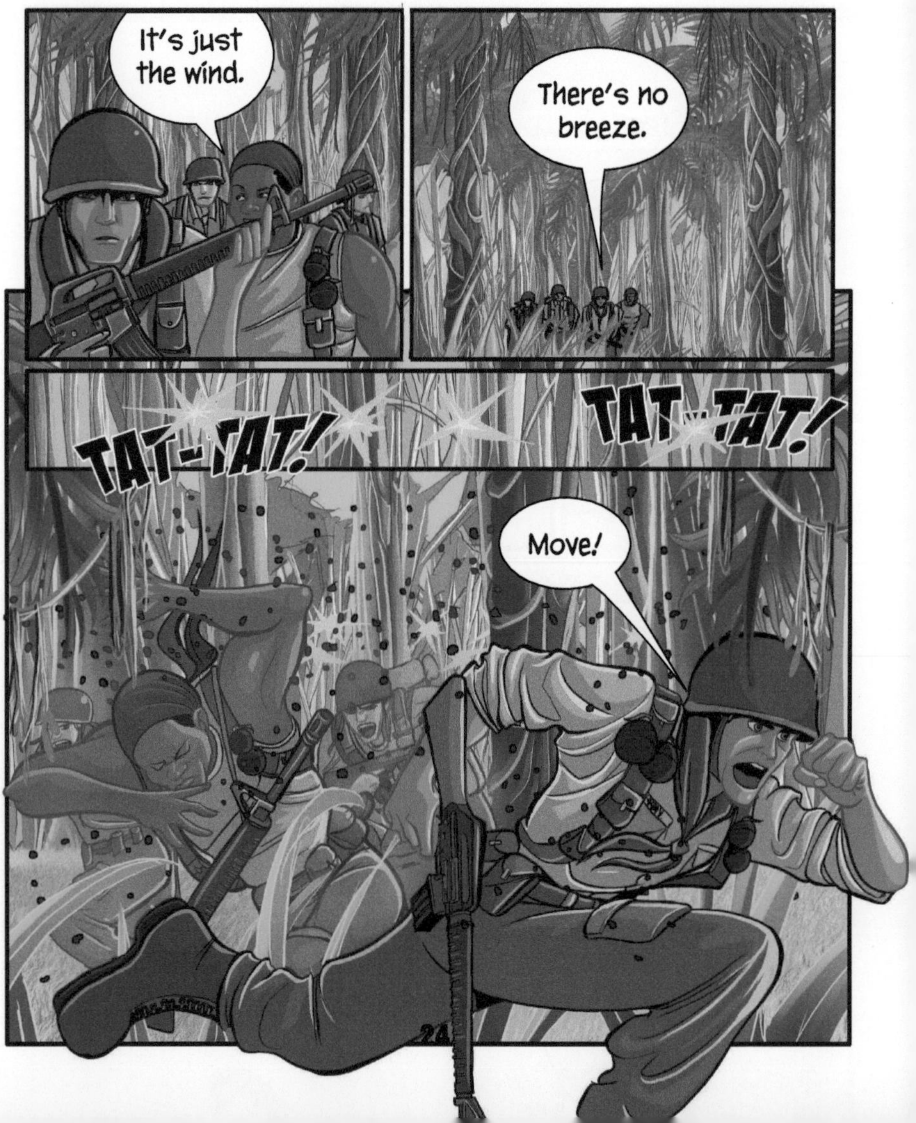
It's just the wind.
There's no breeze.
TAT-TAT!
TAT-TAT!
Move!

The soldiers got to their feet and took off. Shots cracked behind them as they ran. Bullets whizzed past their ears, and rang out against their helmets. Tom's breath was fast. His heart pounded. His feet hurt with every step. Suddenly, Pete was down.

Shot? Tom didn't know. He dove to the ground and crawled on his belly toward his partner.

He couldn't leave him to die in this jungle. Bullets flew overhead. Tom heard them tear through the brush.

"Are you hit?" he asked Pete.

"Not yet," Pete replied.

"Let's get moving," Tom said, getting to his knees.

Pete shook his head. "No more running," he said. "I'm not dying from a shot in the back like a coward."

Pete got to his knees and aimed his rifle. Tom smirked and did the same. They let round after round fly into the jungle. Branches fell, leaves flew, and the Viet Cong returned fire.

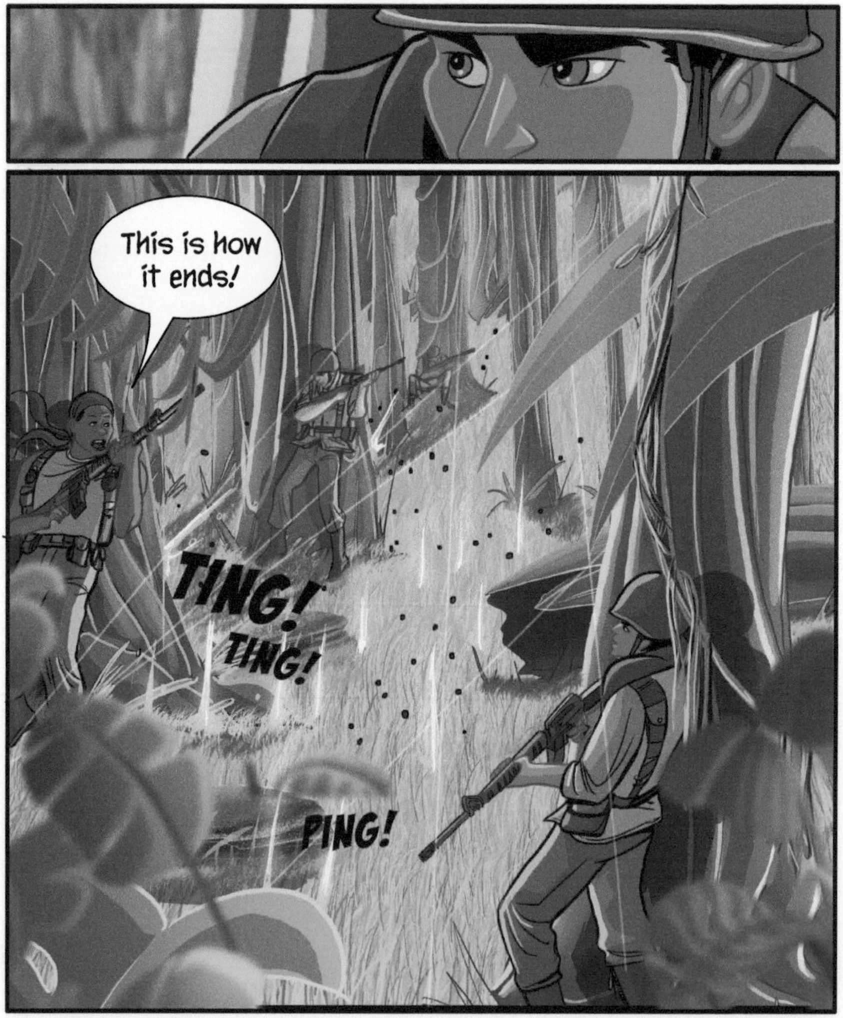
This is how it ends!
TING!
TING!
PING!

Chapter 4

A TRUSTED FRIEND

Pete, Tom, and the other members of the platoon continued firing into the jungle. Then suddenly, something tugged Pete's shirt from behind. He spun around, expecting to stare into the barrel of the enemy's gun.

"Tom!" Pete shouted. "It's the kid!"

Lam Hung saw that the men were surprised, but he had never left them. He had followed the troops and watched the enemy surround them. He knew there was only one way out of this mess.

"Follow me!" he said, in the best English he could speak.

"We should follow him! No arguments!" Tom called out to the troops. Pete nodded.

The soldiers turned and followed the kid through the jungle. Somehow, he led them past the circle of Viet Cong. But they weren't out of danger. Wherever they ran, the enemy followed.

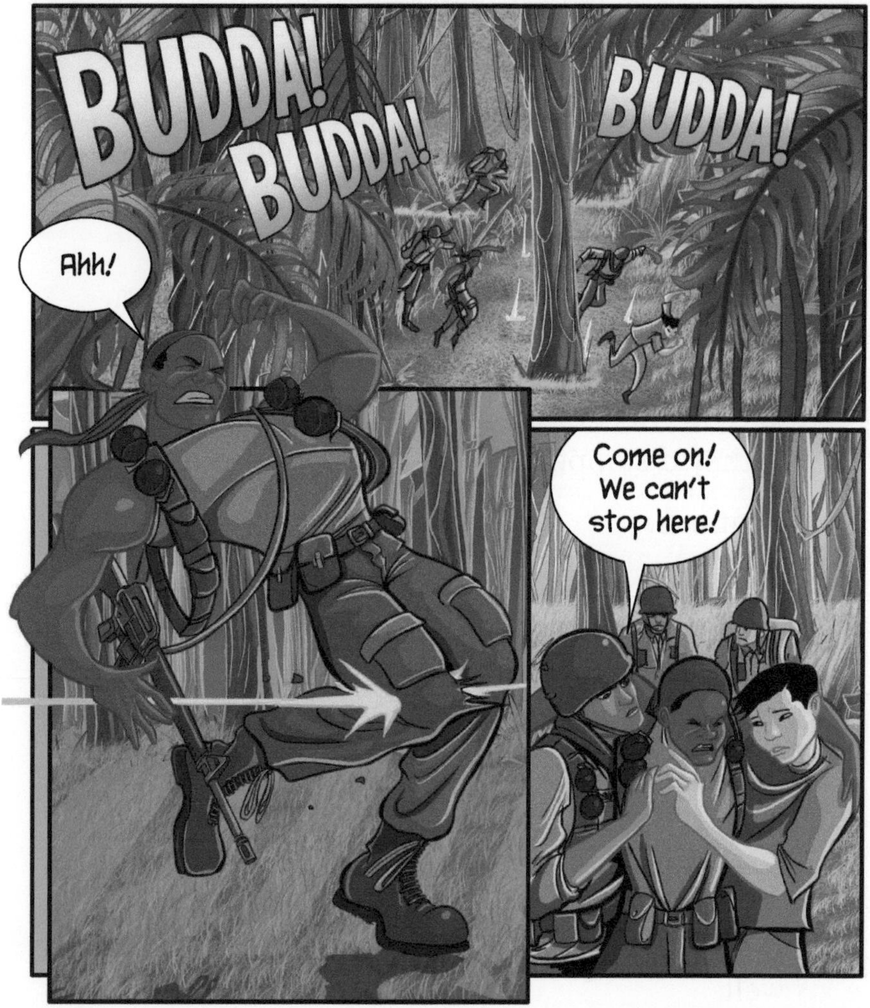
BUDDA! BUDDA!
BUDDA!
Ahh!
Come on! We can't stop here!

The platoon ran on until the sound of AK-47 rifles had faded to silence. Finally, Lam Hung put up his hands to stop. He looked over at Pete and could tell he was hurt. Blood had stained the soldier's pants red from the knee down.

Lam Hung pulled a piece of cloth from his pocket. He pressed it against the bloody spot. He had to stop the bleeding.

The bullet wound was only the first problem. The wound had left a trail of blood through the jungle. To the Viet Cong, the blood would be like a road map toward the American troops.

Pete screamed. "It hurts!"

"Can you keep moving?" Tom asked, kneeling.

Lam Hung pressed the cloth against the bullet hole. Pete shook his head and gritted his teeth.

"The VC will find us in no time if we stay here," Tom said.

"Radio the base," Pete yelled through the pain. "Get the rescue chopper here before we're surrounded again!"

Lam Hung watched the radio operator of the platoon fiddle with the knobs on the field radio. Finally, the operator gave the thumbs up. The rescue helicopter was on the way.

Lam Hung knew the rescue would take time. Meanwhile, they would need a place to hide. They would also need to find an area for the chopper to land. In the middle of the jungle, that could be almost impossible.

He got up and looked around. Then, Lam Hung signaled for the troops to follow him.

"You and the kid go on and save yourselves," Pete said, looking down at his leg. "I can't move too far."

"No way," said Tom. "I'm not leaving you."

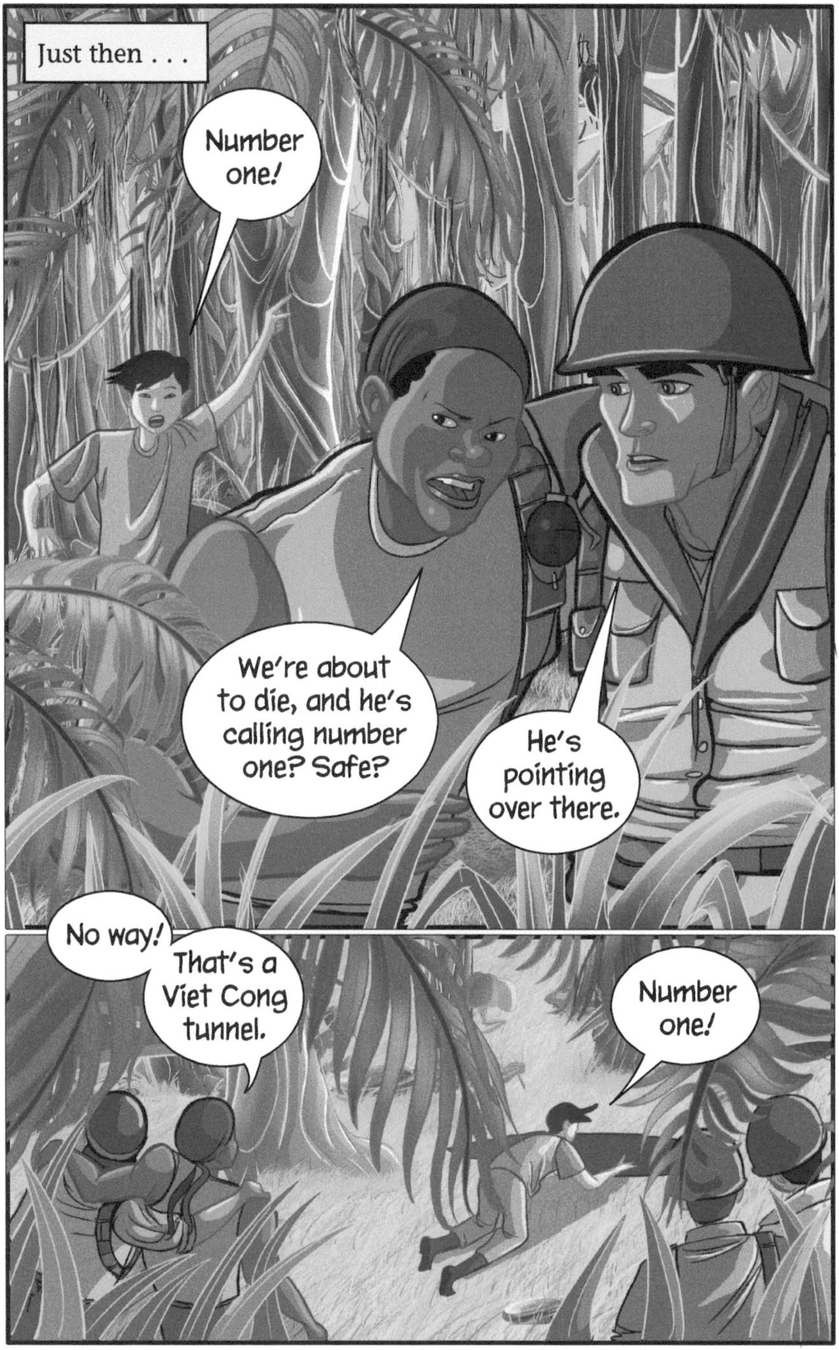
Just then . . .
Number one!
We're about to die, and he's calling number one? Safe?
He's pointing over there.
No way!
That's a Viet Cong tunnel.
Number one!

"That's our only option," Tom said, looking into the mouth of the darkened tunnel.

"I still don't trust this kid," Pete said.

"I trust him," Tom replied. "So trust me."

Lam Hung bent down for a closer look. He knew that the Viet Cong had built thousands of tunnels beneath the jungle floor. They used them to hide from and ambush the American troops. Lam Hung had been inside of them before. He knew that many of the tunnels were too small for American men. He hoped this one would be large enough to keep them all safe.

"Smoke it out," Pete said, handing Lam Hung a grenade.

"No!" yelled Tom. He grabbed the grenade back from the kid. "The Viet Cong will hear the explosion!"

"Then the kid goes in first," said Pete.

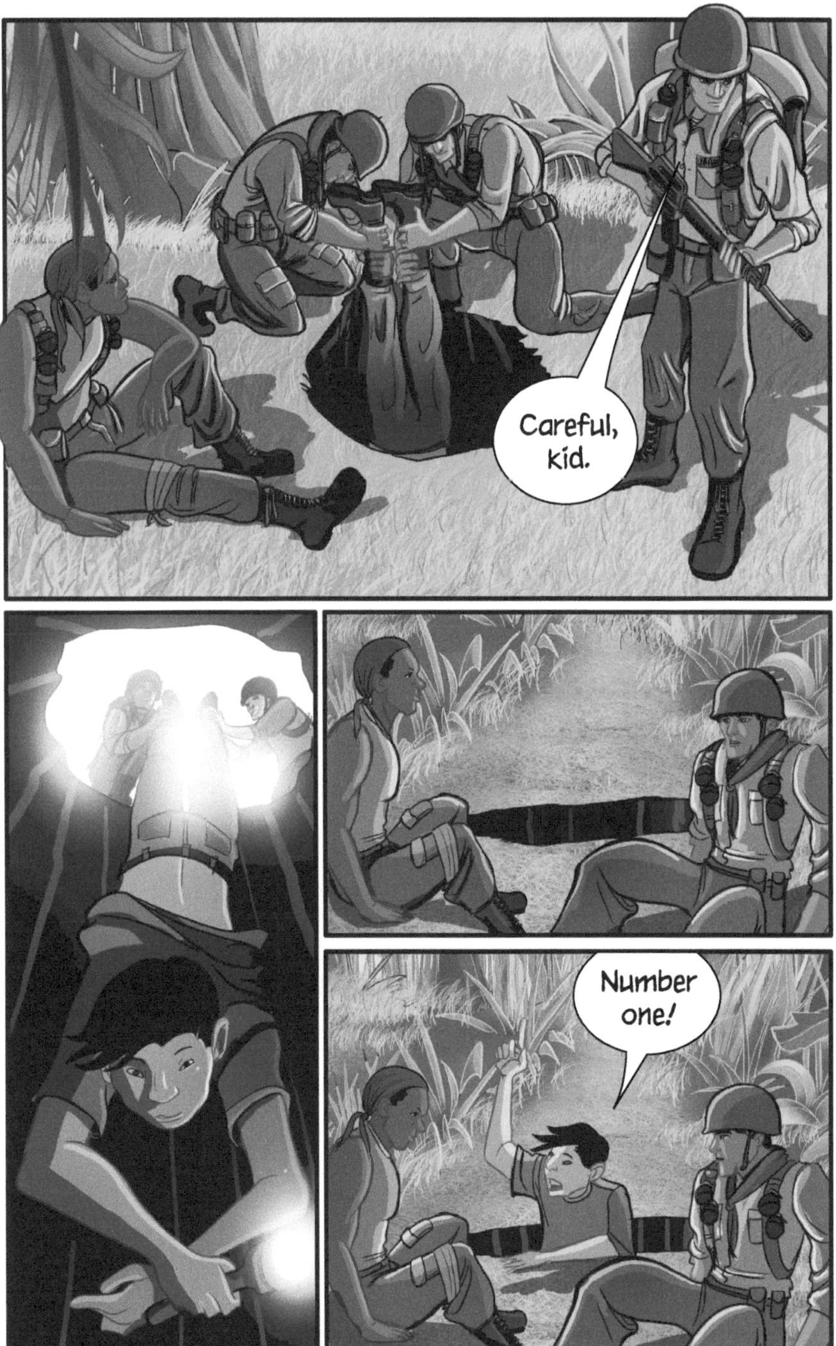
Careful, kid.
Number one!

After Lam Hung had checked the tunnel, the platoon squeezed into the narrow opening. Tom watched from inside the Viet Cong tunnel. He saw the kid sweep the area in front of the tunnel. He was hiding their trail and erasing the drops of blood from Pete's leg wound. Then the kid moved the bush back in front of the mouth of the tunnel.

It was dark and silent. Hung wished it wasn't so quiet. Soon, though, he prayed for the silence. He heard voices coming from outside the tunnel.

"VC," Pete whispered. Tom held up his hand to quiet him. The voices were definitely Viet Cong. They moved closer. Lam Hung could hear their footsteps. The VC had gathered outside the hole.

Tom held his breath. He listened to Pete at his side. His partner's breathing sounded like a hurricane. He was sure the Viet Cong would hear them. He was sure they were doomed.

But the Viet Cong didn't hear him. The voices got quieter, and the footsteps moved away. Lam Hung let out his breath in a sigh.

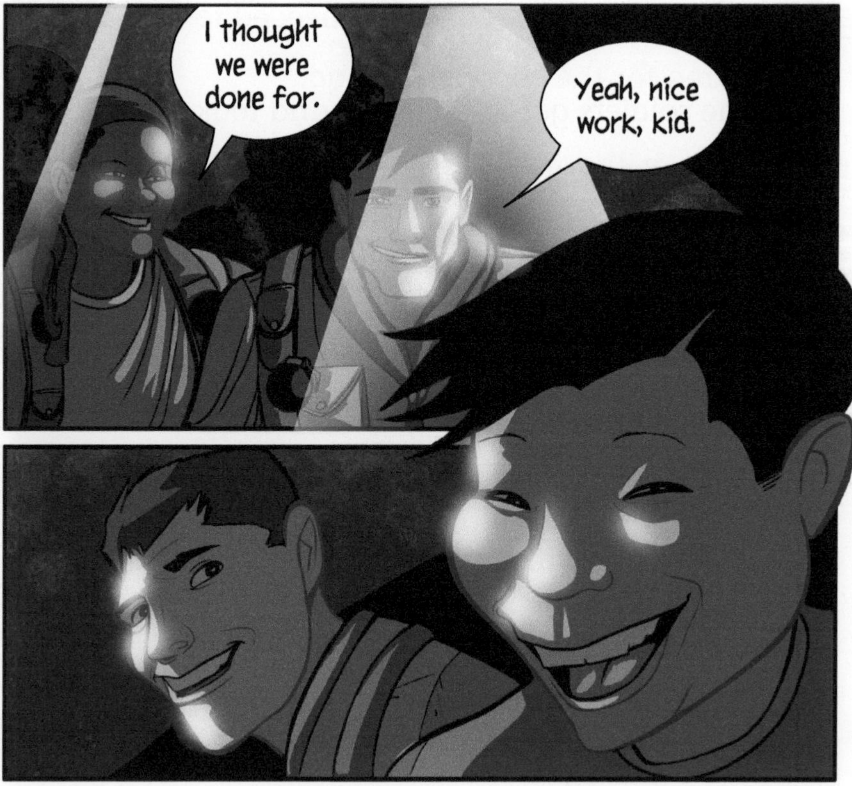
I thought we were done for.
Yeah, nice work, kid.

Chapter 5

NUMBER ONE SOLDIER

Lam Hung helped the soldiers from the tunnel. Then he went off into the jungle to find some wood and small vines. He knew the Viet Cong would be back soon, and they needed to find a safe area for the chopper to land.

Soon, Lam Hung returned with an armful of supplies. He placed them near Pete and started working.

"What's he doing?" Pete asked. He looked up at Tom. His leg was worse, and he couldn't even stand up.

The platoon stood silent, watching Lam Hung work. When he was finished, he pointed at Pete.

"Would you look at that?!" exclaimed Tom.

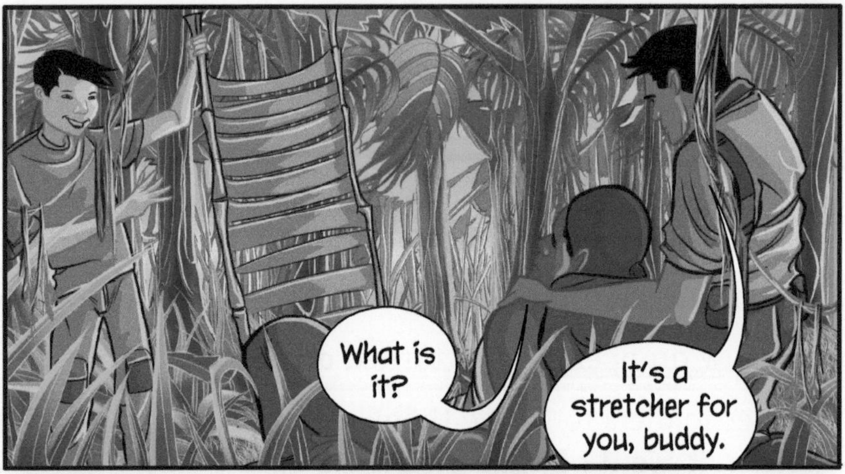
What is it?
It's a stretcher for you, buddy.

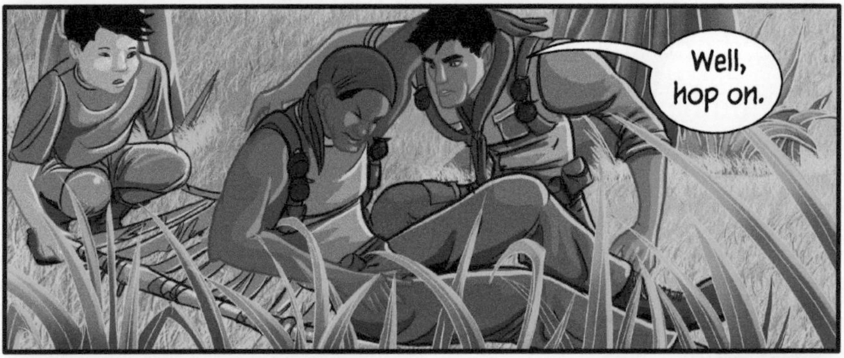
Well, hop on.

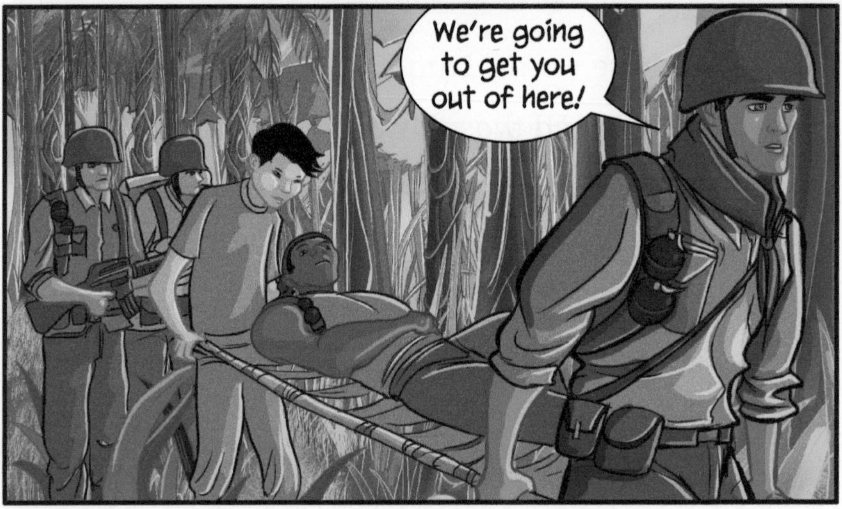
We're going to get you out of here!

Pete didn't argue. Tom and Lam Hung helped him onto the stretcher. They carried him along a thin trail, which passed through the thickest part of the jungle. In the distance, Lam Hung thought he saw an opening. He turned and waved for the other soldiers to follow them.

"The VC went that way!" Tom said, looking in the direction Lam Hung was pointing.

Just then, Tom felt a hand grab his wrist. Pete was looking up at him from the stretcher and nodding. "I trust him this time," he said. "With my life."

With those words, Lam Hung continued on down the trail. He wasn't worried about the Viet Cong anymore. He could hear the rescue chopper in the distance and knew the enemy would keep away for a while. Lam Hung was more worried about what the VC might have left behind. He knew the area was covered in booby traps.

Lam Hung thought following the Viet Cong trail would be their best chance at getting out of the jungle alive. He tried to stay close to their path. He looked for footprints and broken twigs along the way. If the enemy had already walked through the area, he knew it would be safe.

As they walked, the platoon members could hear the chopper getting closer to the clearing. Some of them began to run. Lam Hung knew this wasn't a good idea.

"Come on! It's safe!" one of the soldiers yelled, sprinting ahead down the path.

Lam Hung looked at the ground ahead of him. He could see the Viet Cong footprints in the mud. Then, all of a sudden, the footprints stopped.

"Number ten!" Lam Hung yelled out, pointing ahead on the trail. The soldier didn't stop. Tom dropped the stretcher and sprinted after him.

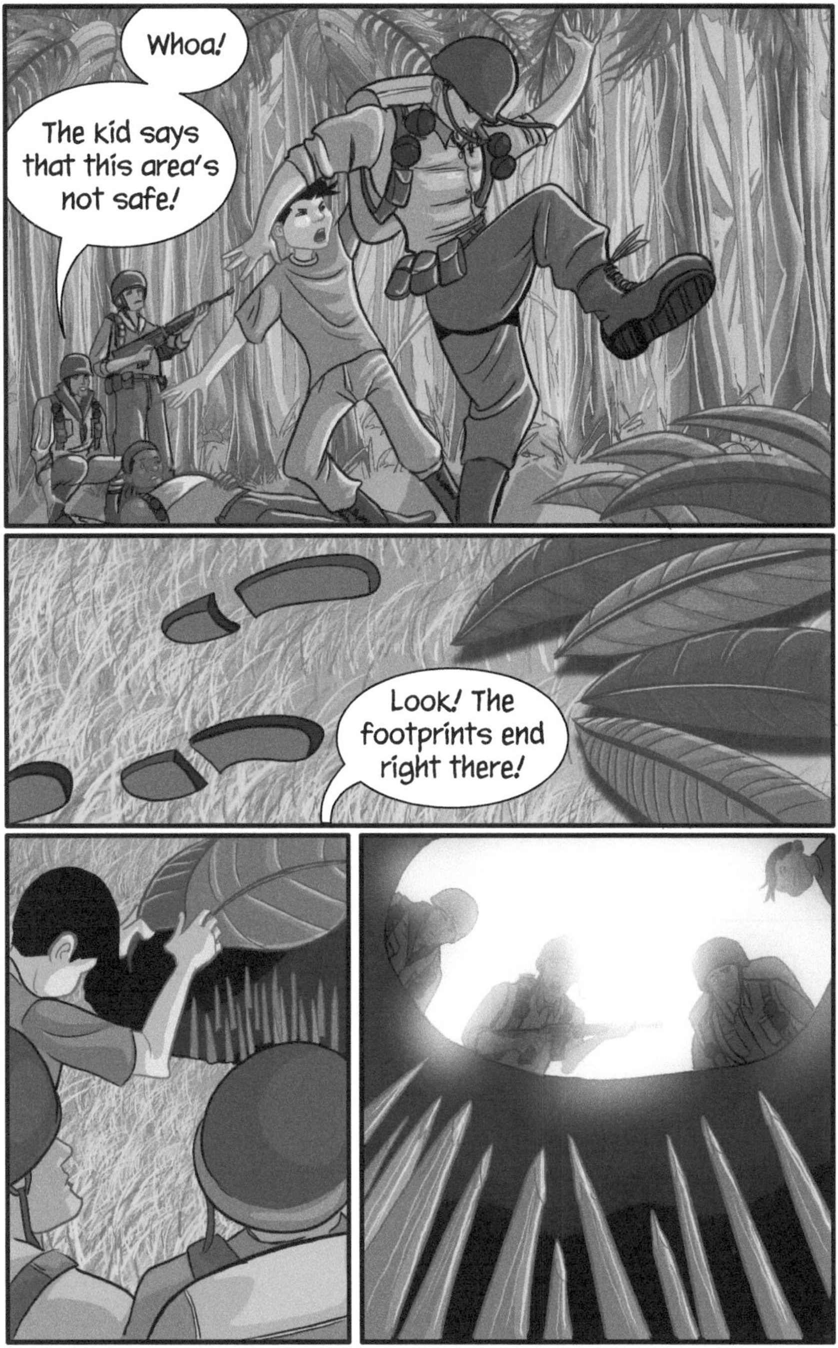
Whoa!
The kid says that this area's not safe!
Look! The footprints end right there!

"One more step and you'd be on a stretcher like me," said Pete, looking into the pit.

The platoon had seen this type of booby trap before. Falling into a spike pit meant injury or even worse.

"Looks like the kid saved us again," said Tom.

Pete looked up from his stretcher. He still couldn't move his leg, but he knew they were getting closer to safety. "Yeah, thanks, Lam Hung," he said.

Lam Hung smiled and nodded. It was the first time the soldiers had used his real name.

The troops walked carefully around the pit and continued on. When they were safely past the booby trap, Lam Hung could see a clear path through the trees to an opening in the distance. Still, he kept his eyes peeled for more booby traps and for the enemy.

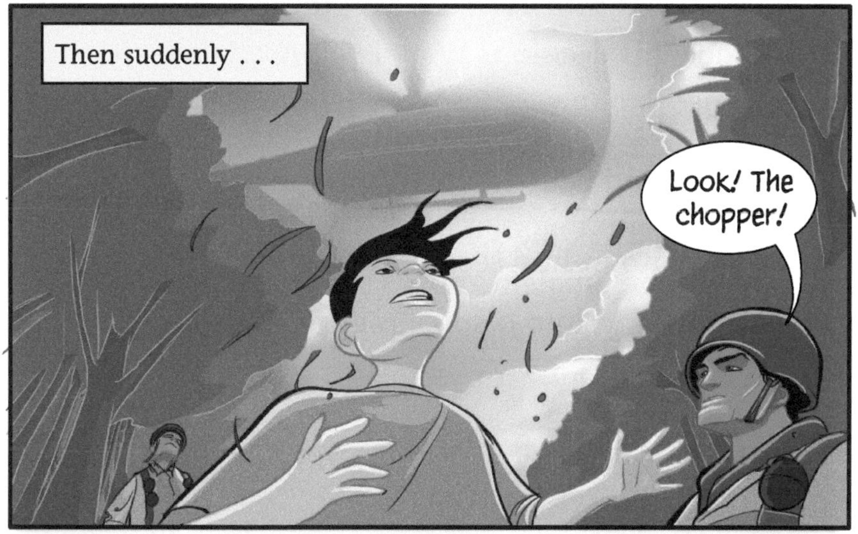
Then suddenly . . .
Look! The chopper!

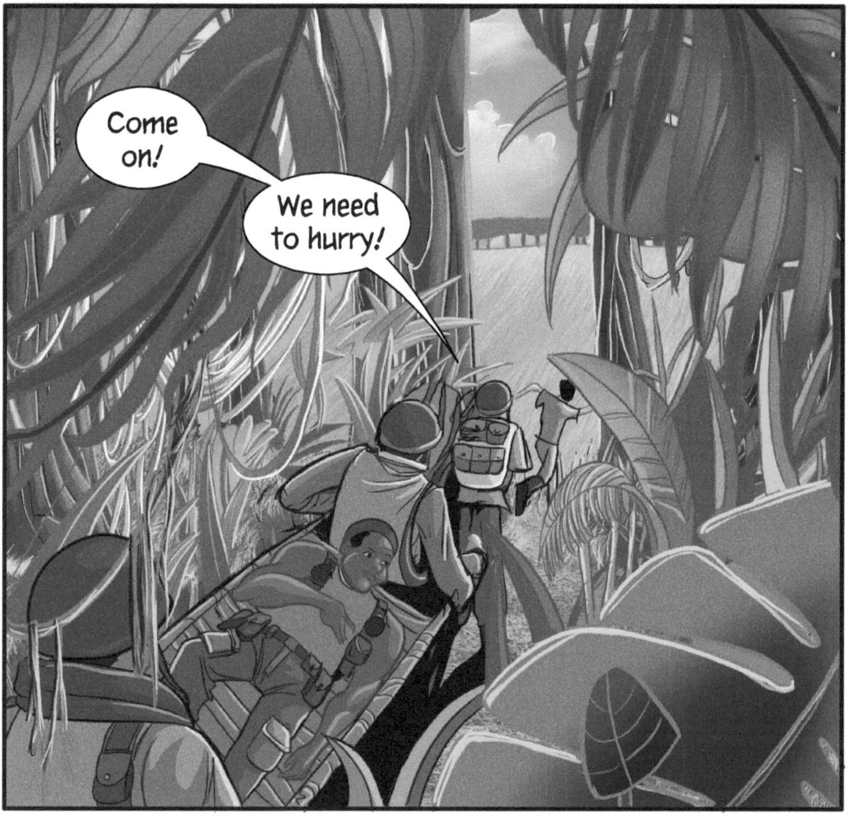
Come on!
We need to hurry!

Suddenly, gunfire burst out of the trees. *Rat-ta-tat! Rat-ta-tat! Rat-ta-tat!* The men kept running.

"The Viet Cong!" yelled Pete. "They're back!"

Lam Hung kept his eyes on the trail ahead as shots whizzed past his head. He pulled the stretcher as quickly as he could.

"Lam Hung! Take this!" Pete handed Lam Hung a signal flare. "Run ahead and alert the chopper that we're here."

Lam Hung was afraid to leave the platoon. He was afraid to leave Tom and Pete behind. But he also knew what he had to do.

He sprinted ahead, running so fast that he couldn't hear the guns firing. As he approached the opening, Lam Hung snapped off the end of the flare. A thick trail of orange smoke streamed behind him. He could see the helicopter passing overhead and hoped it wasn't too late.

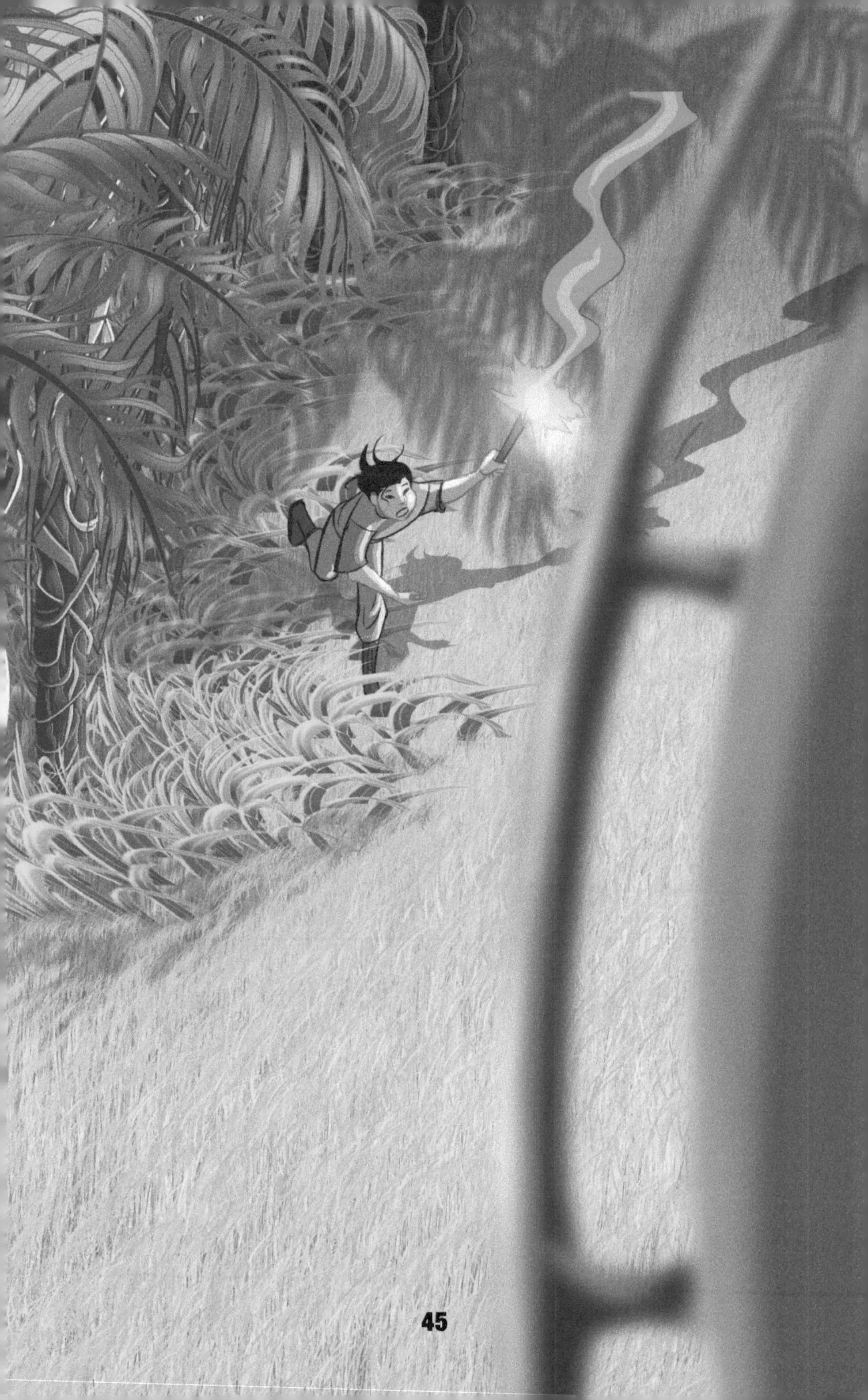

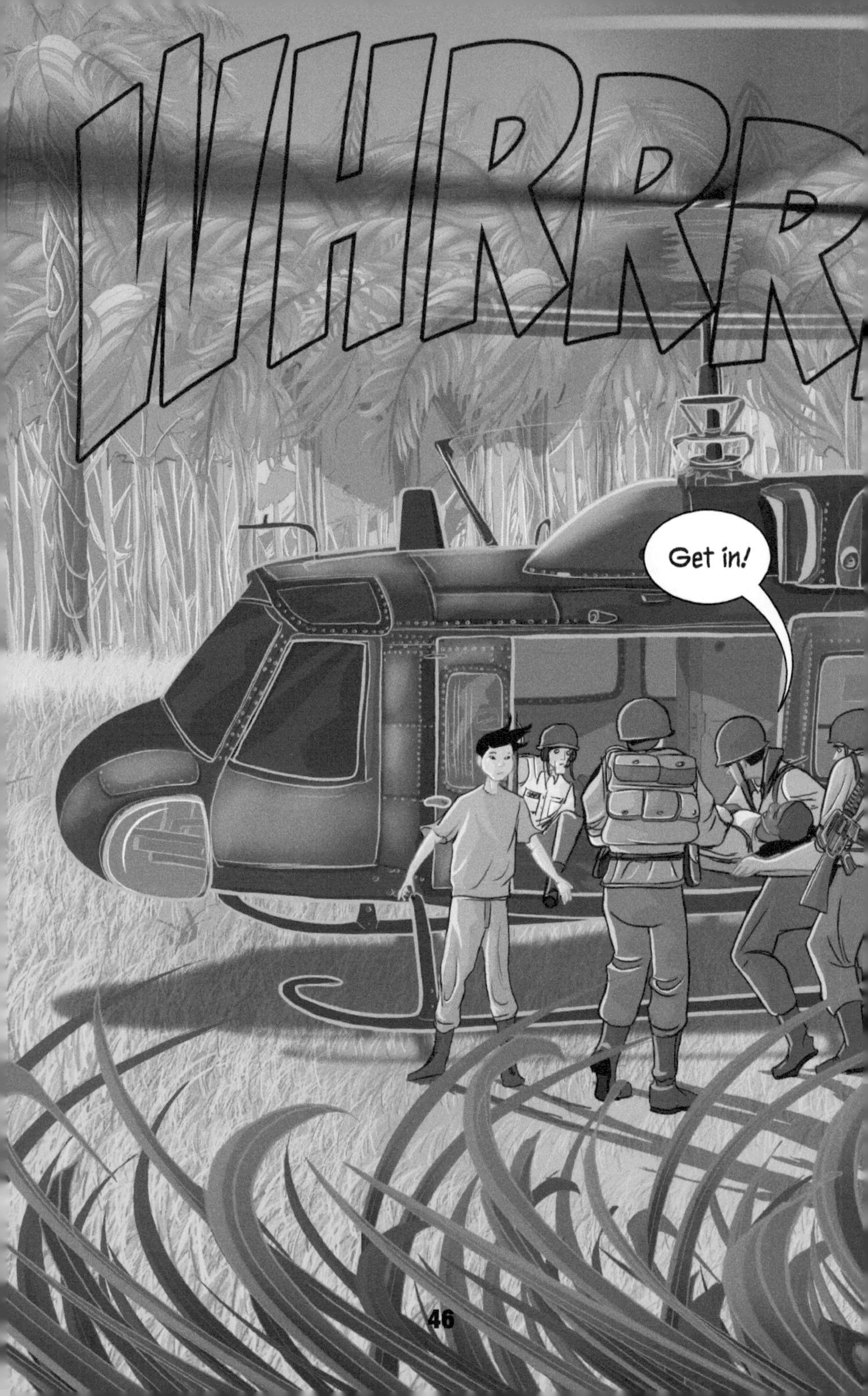
WHRR
Get in!

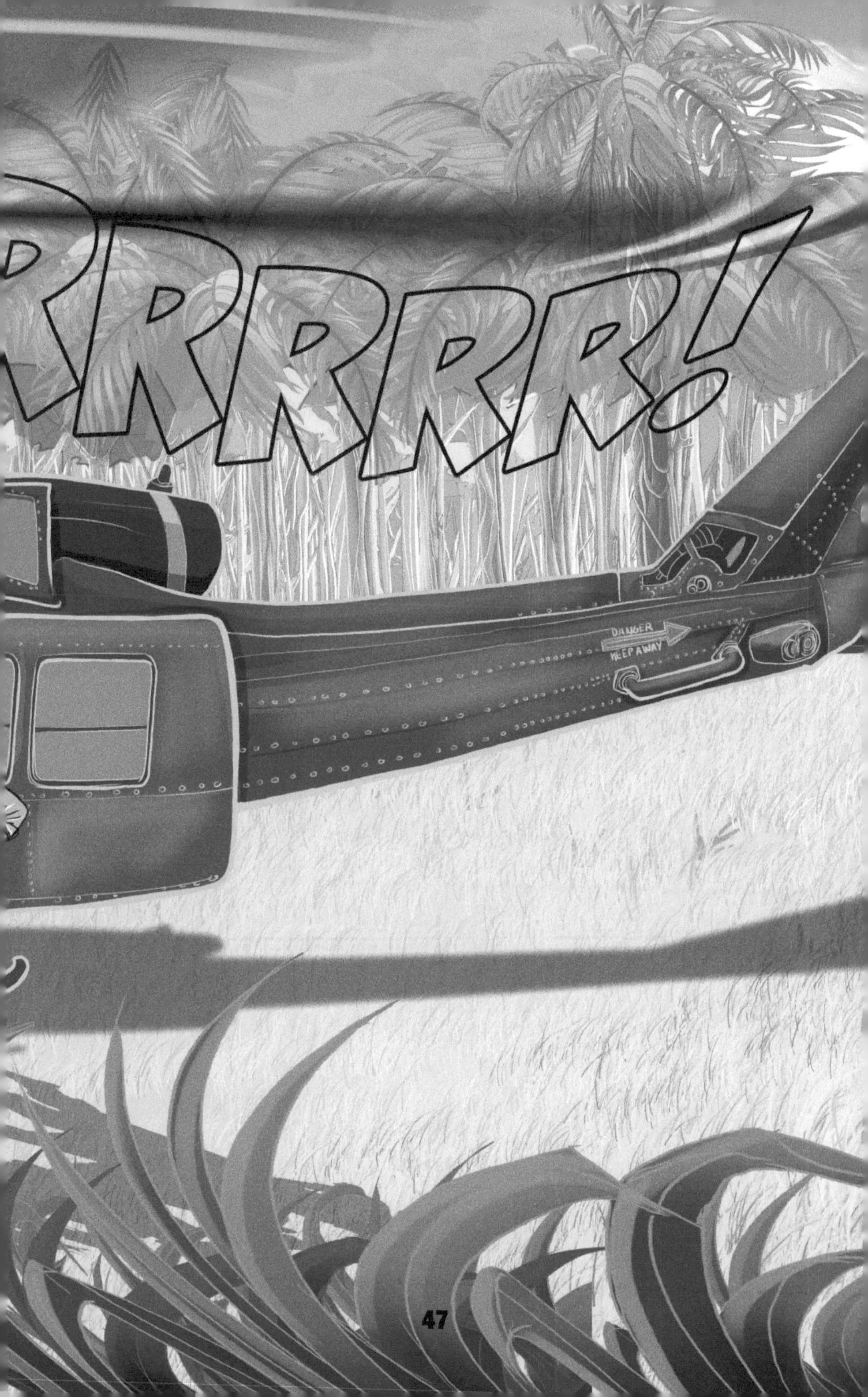
RRRRR!
DANGER
KEEP AWAY

Once inside the helicopter, Pete leaned back against the seat and pulled a can of rations from his pack. He tossed it to Lam Hung.

Lam Hung peeled off the top, scooped out a bite, and ate it. This wasn't lima beans. He smiled. Pete laughed as he watched their scout enjoy his first can of meatloaf.

"You gave him your favorite?" Tom said. "You won't even let me have a meatloaf!"

Pete shrugged and watched the kid eat. After one bite, the kid raised one finger.

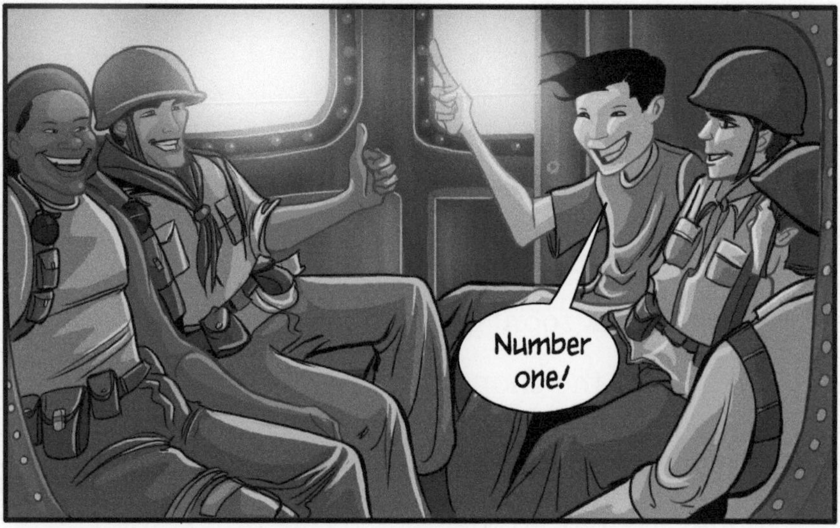
Number one!

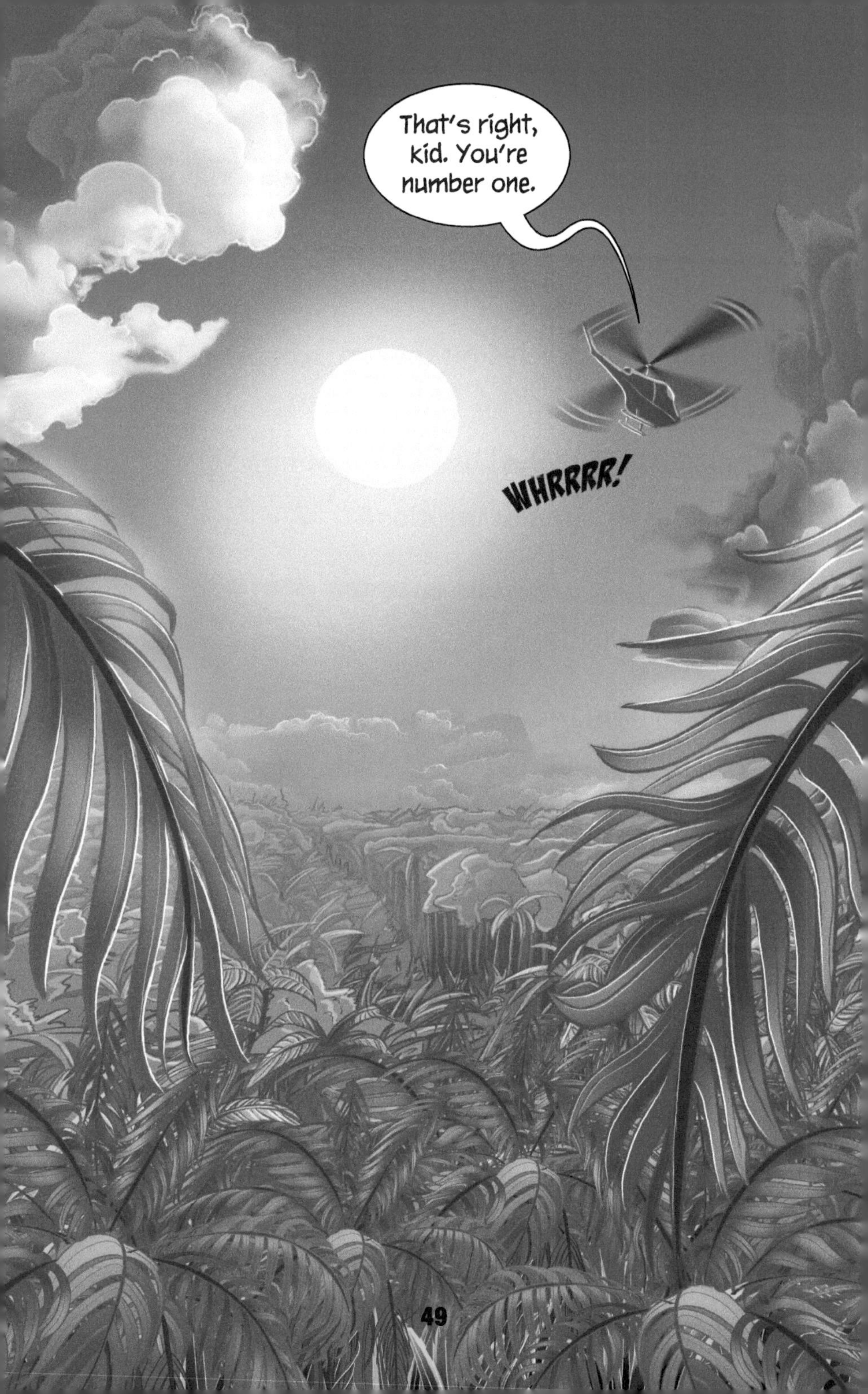
That's right, kid. You're number one.
WHRRRR!

ABOUT THE AUTHOR

Tim Hoppey was born and raised on Long Island in New York. For more than 20 years, he has worked as a New York City firefighter in the neighborhood of East Harlem. In his spare time, Hoppey has written several children's books, including *Tito, The Firefighter* published by Raven Tree Press. He lives with his wife, Ellen, their three kids, and a 14-year-old cat named Scarlet.

ABOUT THE ILLUSTRATOR

Ramon Espinoza (ess-pih-NO-zah) was born in Mexico in 1978. Espinoza grew up reading comics, and at age 20 enrolled in a fine art school. Since graduating, he has worked as an animator, colorist, and storyboard artist for advertisements and short films. He has published comic strips in *Switch* magazine, as well as short stories for *Max* and *FHM* magazines. Espinoza currently lives in Mexico with his wife, Caro, and his dog, Bondi.

GLOSSARY

booby trap (BOO-bee TRAP)—a dangerous trap or weapon that usually is triggered when touched

Communist (KOM-yuh-nist)—the political party of the former Soviet Union; Communist countries usually follow a single leader who controls all the country's land, houses, and businesses.

platoon (plah-TOON)—a small unit of military soldiers

rations (RASH-uhnz)—a food supply given to soldiers for a single day of combat

snipers (SNYP-uhrz)—members of the military who can shoot long distances, usually from hidden locations

stretcher (STRECH-ur)—a device used for carrying a sick or injured person

Viet Cong (vee-ET KONG)—a group of soldiers who fought to make North and South Vietnam one Communist country during the Vietnam War

Vietnam (vee-et-NAHM)—a country in southeast Asia. During the Vietnam War (1959–1975), the country was divided into North and South Vietnam.

MORE ABOUT THE VIETNAM WAR

The war in Vietnam started long before the U.S. military arrived. For more than 100 years, France had ruled the southeast Asian country. In July 1945, Vietnamese troops forced the French out. Afterward, the nations agreed that Vietnam would be divided in half for the next two years.

The United States government, however, did not think the two parts should reunite. They believed Communist leaders in the northern part of Vietnam would gain too much power. Instead, the United States decided to help the southern part create a new country called South Vietnam.

The government of North Vietnam did not agree with this decision. From 1958–1960, they tried to take over the government of South Vietnam. After political attempts failed, North Vietnam decided to attack South Vietnam. Other Communist countries, such as China and Russia, helped them with supplies and weapons. A group of Communists in South Vietnam helped with the fighting. They were known as the Viet Cong.

The United States government wanted to end this spread of Communism. In 1965, President Lyndon Johnson sent the first combat troops into the region. Others soon followed. By the end of 1966, more than 385,000 American soldiers were in Vietnam. While there, these men and women faced many challenges, including hot weather, thick jungles, and a growing Viet Cong army.

The tough conditions made the war difficult to win. Many U.S. soldiers died, and Americans wanted the fighting to stop. On January 27, 1973, the United States signed a peace agreement with North Vietnam, ending America's longest war.

During the Vietnam War, 58,195 American soldiers were killed. In 1982, they were honored with the Vietnam Veterans Memorial in Washington, D.C. Visitors to the monument can read all the soldiers' names, which have been carved into the monument wall.

DISCUSSION QUESTIONS

1. Why didn't Pete and some of the other U.S. soldiers trust Lam Hung? Do you think it was fair that the soldiers didn't trust him? Why or why not?

2. Even though Pete didn't like him, Lam Hung saved Pete's life. Why do you think Lam Hung made this decision? Would you have done the same? Explain.

3. Do you think the soldiers could have gotten out of the jungle without Lam Hung? What skills did Lam Hung have that helped the platoon survive?

WRITING PROMPTS

1. This story is known as historical fiction. The historical event is true, but the characters are fiction. Choose your favorite historical event. Then make up a story that happens on that day.

2. At the end of the story, Lam Hung and the soldiers get out of the jungle. What will happen next? Will Lam Hung get an award for his bravery? Will he return to the jungle to fight again? Write it down.

3. Write your own war story and make yourself the main character. Would you be a soldier, a commander, or maybe a medical doctor? Use your imagination.

INTERNET SITES

Do you want to know more about subjects related to this book? Or are you interested in learning about other topics? Then check out FactHound, a fun, easy way to find Internet sites.

Our investigative staff has already sniffed out great sites for you!

Here's how to use FactHound:

1. Visit *www.facthound.com*

2. Select your grade level.

3. To learn more about subjects related to this book, type in the book's ISBN number: 9781434207470.

4. Click the Fetch It button.

FactHound will fetch the best Internet sites for you.